## #2
# PEANUT AND JILLY FOREVER

## Dorothy Haas

Illustrated by Jeffrey Lindberg

A
**LITTLE APPLE**
PAPERBACK

SCHOLASTIC INC.
New York Toronto London Auckland Sydney

*For the VanderVoorts:*
*Steve, Nicole, Lise, and Nina.*

ISBN 0-590-41507-7

12 11 10 9 8 7 6 5 4 3 2           8 9/8 0 1 2 3/9

Printed in the U.S.A.       11

First Scholastic printing, September 1988

# CHAPTER
# 1

▀▄▀▄▀▄▀▄▀▄▀▄▀▄▀▄▀▄▀▄▀▄▀

Things were not going well.

What exactly was Jilly to think of that new girl, Peanut? She talked, talked, talked all the time. About wonderful Minneapolis. About wonderful Regan. About wonderful Halverson School.

And Peanut — what was she to think of that girl Jilly in her class at Louisa May Alcott School? She hardly said anything, even when Peanut did her best to make her talk. Then, when she did break down, all she talked about was the wonderful Blue Rose, the wonderful Balloon Blast-Off contest.

That Peanut! thought Jilly. So, all right — she had read a hundred and two books. So what! Some of the books were probably for babies, with more pictures than words.

That Jilly! thought Peanut. Okay — she had read a hundred and three books. Big deal! She had probably skipped all the hard parts.

Jilly was proud of her vocabulary cards. She had the best words, like *serendipity*. That one meant finding good things by accident, just stumbling on them. She liked saying it aloud: "Sehr-en-DIP-ih-tee." Nobody in Miss Kraft's class had ever found a longer word. It had eleven letters. Eleven!

Peanut had vocabulary cards, too. She had brought them with her from Minneapolis. Her best word was a mouthful — *tintinnabulation*. She said it meant bells ringing and taught everybody to say it: "Tin-tinn-ab-u-LAY-shun." There were sixteen letters in it!

When she told everybody that, she stared right at Jilly. Jilly stared back, pretending not to care.

Miss Kraft looked from Peanut to Jilly. But she didn't say anything.

One day Miss Kraft asked who knew the capital city of Canada.

Peanut's and Jilly's hands shot up before anybody else's did. Waggling their fingers at Miss Kraft, they glared at each other.

I bet Jilly doesn't really know it's Montreal, thought Peanut. She was sure the answer was Montreal.

I bet Peanut doesn't know for sure it's Toronto, thought Jilly. She was certain the capital of Canada was Toronto.

Miss Kraft saw them glaring at each other. She looked tired and let out her breath in a long sigh. Then she called on David.

"Ottawa," said David. "They have a building there just like one in London. We spent our vacation in Canada and we watched the changing of the guard. My mom said it was exactly like London."

"Excellent, David," said Miss Kraft. "You are absolutely right."

Ottawa! Peanut and Jilly dropped their eyes to their books.

In art class, Jilly drew flowers that looked as though they were just waiting to be picked.

When they sang, Peanut's voice lifted high and sweet over everyone else's.

When they played basketball, Jilly dropped the most baskets.

In soccer games, Peanut always made the most goals.

"I'm better than she is. . . ."

"I can do anything she can do. I can do it better. . . ."

"Can't. . . ."

"Can. . . ."

"We'll just see. . . ."

"Hah!"

"Who needs her?"

Sometimes Miss Kraft sighed when she looked at Peanut and Jilly. At times she closed her eyes and rubbed her forehead as though she had a headache.

No, things were not going well with Polly Butterman and Jillian Matthews.

One day the class went downstairs to the arts and crafts room to get the bowls they had made. Mr. Fortunato, the art teacher, had taken them out of the kiln and set them on the table in the center of the room. Everyone bumped elbows finding their bowls.

Jilly's bowl felt wonderful in her hands — smooth and cool. When it was held just right, a person could hardly see that it sagged a little on one side. It was the most heavenly blue.

Peanut turned her bowl around and around, pleased and proud. The shape was perfect, and it had scarcely any queer bumps on it. It was the most glorious crimson color.

Jilly looked from her blue bowl to Peanut's red one. "Miss Kraft's favorite color is blue," she said.

Peanut ran a finger around the rim of her red bowl. "I think red is her favorite color. She has that red leather jacket and those red coral beads."

Jilly shook her head. "Blue," she said.

"Red," said Peanut in a voice that wouldn't be pushed around.

"Blue."

"Red."

"Let's ask her."

"You'll see."

"No, you'll see."

"Let's not tell her who made which bowl."

"Let's see which one she likes best."

Peanut's and Jilly's eyes danced. Each one thought she knew which bowl Miss Kraft would choose, which she would like best.

They were the first ones out of the arts and crafts room. Dashing upstairs, they set the bowls on Miss Kraft's desk and sat down to wait.

Soon everyone else came tumbling through the door, and Miss Kraft closed it behind them.

"All right, people," she called over the racket, "put your bowls on the windowsills until it's time to go home."

There was a scramble to and from the windows. When everyone returned to their desks, the windowsills were lined with bright bowls of every shape and size.

"We're going to start a new project," said Miss Kraft. "It's about animals and writing. Each of you is going to choose an animal and read all about it and then write about it as though you were that animal. You will — " Her eyes rested on the bowls on her desk. "I thought I told you to put these on the windowsills. Polly, isn't this your bowl? And Jillian. . . . "

She looked from Peanut to Jilly. "Well now," she said as though she understood something they didn't. She picked up the two bowls at exactly the same time and set them on the bookshelves behind her desk. "We'll talk about this later," she said. "For now, let's get on with our animal reports."

And then they started thinking about animals.

7

# CHAPTER
## 2

■▼■▼■▼■▼■▼■▼■▼■▼■▼■▼■▼■

"I'm going to be a squirrel," burbled Erin. "I love the way they bounce around and — " She clapped her hands over her mouth. "Oh, I forgot!"

"You're not supposed to tell your animal, Dumbo," said Ollie, rolling his eyes. "At the end of the project we're gonna divide into teams and guess who chose what animal."

Emmy's eyes flashed. "Don't you call Erin Dumbo, Ollie," she said. "Honestly, you've got such a mouth! You can choose to be a hippo — they've got such big mouths they eat a bushel of stuff in one gulp."

Erin looked contrite. "I'll pick another animal," she said. "And I'll remember not to tell what it is. But it sure is hard to keep secrets."

Everyone was sitting on the floor around the bookshelves under the windows. They were all being careful to keep the pictures on the pages of their books hidden from each other. Jilly had the En–Fi book of the encyclopedia. Peanut was reading the Do–Em book.

"Polly? Jillian?" called Miss Kraft. "May I speak with you for a minute?"

Hugging their books, Peanut and Jilly went to her desk.

"Now," said Miss Kraft, looking from one to the other, "I'm wondering why you left your bowls on my desk. Do you want to tell me?"

Peanut and Jilly spoke at the same time. "To find out your favorite color." "To see which one you would choose."

Miss Kraft puffed out her cheeks on a big breath and let it out. "Honestly, you two are driving me to distraction. I have never met a more competitive pair of kids."

Peanut and Jilly stared at their gymshoes.

9

Miss Kraft sounded as though she didn't much like kids who competed with each other.

"You are such nice girls," Miss Kraft went on. "By all odds, you should like each other."

Peanut and Jilly were still. But the looks they sent each other clearly said, "Like *her?*"

"I'm going to hold onto your bowls for a while," said Miss Kraft. "That is, if you don't mind."

Peanut and Jilly shook their heads. They didn't mind.

"Good," said Miss Kraft. "And now I have a special project for the two of you."

Peanut and Jilly looked up, interested. Miss Kraft thought of the best projects of any teacher in school. They were always fun.

"I want you to research each other," said Miss Kraft, "just the way we're researching our animals. And then you will write about each other."

Jilly thought she wasn't hearing right. What was wrong with Miss Kraft, coming up with a terrible project like this? "But there aren't any books about her," she protested, pointing at Peanut. "So how. . . ?" The question hung in the air.

Peanut winced. What a horrible project! She finished Jilly's question. ". . . can we learn about each other without finding stuff in books?"

"You can watch each other," Miss Kraft said blandly. "That's what animal scientists do, you know. And you can interview each other — ask each other questions."

A further dreadful idea came to Peanut. "And then, like the animals project, I'm supposed to write about her like I *am* her?" She looked as though she had just swallowed a fly.

"Exactly," said Miss Kraft, smiling as though this was the most spectacular project she had ever thought of.

The full meaning of all this descended upon Jilly. She thought she was going to throw up. "I can't pretend I'm her!" she moaned.

"Try," said Miss Kraft. "You are both imaginative. Work together on how you are going to do this."

Polly always saw the good side of things. Her face brightened. "Since we're going to write about each other, we don't have to do the animal project. Right?"

"Wrong," said Miss Kraft. "You're doing this one just for fun."

"Why are you punishing us?" asked Jilly, a worried frown on her face. "We haven't done anything bad. We don't fight or anything like that."

Miss Kraft spoke gently. "You haven't done

anything bad at all. This isn't punishment. I think you're going to enjoy this project. As for doing two assignments — you are both able to handle that. You know you can." She turned away. "If you have any questions, come and talk to me."

She went to the book corner to help Elvis, who was giggling helplessly over something in his book.

"I know all about you," said Peanut, looking sideways at Jilly. "I don't need to interview you."

"Well, I know about you, too," said Jilly. "I'm going to write about you right now. So there."

They marched to their desks and plopped down into their seats. Each opened her notebook to a fresh sheet of paper. From time to time they sent black looks at each other.

At the top of her paper, Jilly wrote *My name is Polly Butterman.*

Oh, pickle juice! she thought, resting her cheek on her hand, looking at that name, making a face. Then, crossing out *Polly* and writing *Peanut* above it, she wrote:

People call me Peanut because I'm pretty fat. I have a shape like a peanut. I used to live in wonderful Minneapolis and I went to a wonderful school that was better than Louisa May Alcott. I talk all the time and my other name is Motor Mouth. Someday soon I am going back to Minneapolis.

Peanut chewed on her pencil for a while, thinking. Then she wrote *I am Jilly Matthews* at the top of her paper. The thought was so awful that she had to stop writing for a while. When she got her strength back, she wrote:

I'm so skinny my bones stick out. My hair isn't any color. Maybe the doctor dropped me in a bottle of clothes bleach when I was born. I'm stuck up. I don't talk to people because I'm so smart and nobody is as smart as I am. Maybe someday I'll move away from here and that will be okay.

Peanut and Jilly slid sideways glances at

14

each other. They laid aside their pencils and read what they had written about each other, thinking, Pretty good! and That's just like her! But even while they felt pleased, the worm of another idea wriggled into their thoughts. Each thought of reading what the other had written. Peanut began to squirm. Jilly huddled into herself.

After a long moment, Peanut folded her paper and stuffed it into her pocket. Jilly made an origami bird out of hers and pushed it into her backpack.

They were going to have to interview each other after all.

The bell rang and everyone rushed out of the room, glad to be out of school for the day.

Emmy and Erin were walking home together. Jilly fell into step with them. After a moment, so did Peanut.

"I've read all about — " Erin started to say.

Emmy clapped her hand over Erin's mouth. "You've got to keep it a secret this time."

Erin pulled away, giggling. "I was only going to say I read all about Halloween today. I'm going to be an alien creature this year. And I won't forget and tell about my animal. Honest I won't."

"I'm going to write some questions tonight," said Peanut, looking at Jilly. "I'll ask you tomorrow."

"I'll write some questions, too," said Jilly.

They were glum. What a terrible thing Miss Kraft had done to them.

# CHAPTER
## 3

It was recess and everybody was playing volleyball or kickball. But Peanut and Jilly were sitting on the steps in the golden autumn sunshine, their notebooks open on their knees.

"Okay," said Peanut. "Now this is the like and don't-like part. Do you like oysters?"

Jilly made a face. "Bleah!" Then she added, "I bet you like them."

"Can't stand them," said Peanut.

Jilly was suspicious. "So you thought I would like them?"

"If I may say so," Polly replied huffily, "that's dumb. I just thought it was interesting. I mean,

17

since I was making this list of stupid questions, I thought I might as well put in something to make me laugh."

"Oh," said Jilly. She thought about it. "You know, that was a pretty good question. Did you know that people eat oysters raw?"

"Maybe they're still alive when people swallow them," Peanut said thoughtfully, her eyes widening.

The girls stared at each other in horror.

"Do you suppose they know they're being swallowed?" asked Jilly.

"Maybe they give out these scared little moans," said Peanut.

"If people could hear them moaning, I bet they wouldn't eat any more raw oysters," said Jilly. "I mean, even though they do look yucky, they shouldn't have to die a horrible death. Now it's my turn. Did you ever take dancing lessons?"

"Yes."

"Did you like them?"

"I hated them," Peanut said in a low, intense voice. "My feet kept bumping into each other and my elbows were always wrong, poking

18

into the girls next to me." Her eyes focused on Jilly. "I bet you absolutely adored dancing lessons."

Jilly shook her head until her bangs flopped. "I felt like everybody was staring at me and I wanted to *die*. And then one day everybody did stare, because there was this recital and I was supposed to do some steps by myself. I couldn't remember them, so I just stood there. It was awful."

"Miss Karkow told my mother I probably belonged in modern dance," said Peanut. "I mean, she was nice about it. She didn't say I was terrible."

"My dad told my mom I was the saddest-looking kid he'd ever seen and I shouldn't have to do that anymore. So then I didn't," said Jilly. "Now here's another one. What name are you glad you aren't named?"

Polly thought about it. "Blanche," she said finally. "How about you?"

"Wilhelmina," said Jilly, who had given a lot of thought to this question. "I'm really glad I'm not called Wilhelmina."

The bell rang and everyone came crowding

to the steps, getting into line to go inside. Peanut and Jilly joined them.

They had been working on their project for three days. Whenever they had a few free moments they asked each other questions and wrote the answers in their notebooks.

During free study time, Peanut asked, "What's the very worst thing you ever did?"

Jilly thought for a while. "I was a really little kid," she said finally. "I took my mother's comb and I crawled behind the sofa and broke off almost all of the teeth. I remember they had a really neat bend-y feeling before they popped off." She paused, thinking. "I wonder why I did that." Then she added, "I got spanked. What about you?"

"It was before my father died," said Peanut. "He was doing some work on these really long sheets of paper. It was pretty important. He got up to go do something and left them on the floor beside his chair. I drew some red stick people on them while he was gone. I sort of knew when I was doing it that I wasn't supposed to." She was silent for a moment, a faraway look in her eyes. "I wish I hadn't done that," she said softly.

On their way to the lunchroom, Jilly asked, "What's the scariest thing you can think of?"

"This chalk-white face with glowing red eyes looking in my window at night," said Peanut. "Of course, that's kind of silly, because my bedroom is up on the second floor."

They both laughed.

"You?" asked Peanut. "What's scary for you?"

"Talking to people I don't know," said Jilly. She shuddered. "I always want to just disappear."

"But that's not *scary*," Peanut protested. "You're supposed to say something spooky-scary."

"Yes, it is," said Jilly.

"Isn't," said Peanut.

"Is," said Jilly. "I'd rather . . . rather . . . eat grasshoppers!"

Peanut didn't have an answer for that. Her head tilted to one side, a thoughtful look on her face, she studied Jilly. But she didn't say anything more.

Their notebooks became quite full.

"What's the worst dream you ever had?"

"A giant mouse was chasing me."

"There was this great huge pizza and every time I tried to take a bite it slid away from me."

"What makes you laugh?"

"Being tickled. I hate it."

"Thinking about grown-ups doing silly things. Like Mr. Granger dressed up like a baby waving this big bottle and saying '*Wahhhhh.*' "

"What's the best useless information you've got?"

"If a crab breaks off its claw, it grows a new one."

"That's not useless. It's very important for the crab."

"But not for people. People can't grow a new finger if one breaks off. What's your useless information?"

"Bears don't hibernate."

"They do, too."

"Uh-uh. They just take these really long naps. But they don't get stone-cold like animals that really hibernate. I read that in the encyclopedia just the other day."

"If it was in the encyclopedia it wasn't useless."

"It sure is useless. I can't use it anyway."

That question, about the most useless information, ended in a draw. They couldn't really decide what was useless.

"Want to come to my house?" Peanut asked after school. "I mean, we can ask each other questions while we eat something."

They walked toward home with Emmy and Erin, but they turned at Forest Avenue and continued on their way to the house with the weeping willow in the front yard.

# CHAPTER
# 4

Lilting piano music poured out of the house when Peanut opened the door. But they didn't get any farther than the door. A wriggling bundle of fluff flung itself at Peanut, jumping at her knees, yipping wildly. She scooped it up and looked into eyes that could scarcely be seen under all that hair. "Did you miss me today, Nibbsie?"

The scrap of a dog licked her chin and Peanut laughed. "This is Nibbsie," she said. "My mom calls him His Nibs, but Nibbsie's a better name."

The little dog's excitement was catching,

and Jilly had to laugh. "I thought you said his leg was in a cast," she said, looking but not seeing anything.

"Came off last week," said Peanut. "Now he's as good as new." She held the puppy out so that Jilly could pet him. Nibbsie growled.

"I bet he smells Bumpy on my clothes," said Jilly. "Aw, come on, Nibbsie — I'm not a cat. I'm not going to chase you."

Nibbsie put up with being scratched behind his ears. But he wasn't overly friendly.

"That's my mom playing the piano. Come on," said Peanut, and ambled into the living room. She went to the piano and leaned against it, cuddling Nibbsie. She loved listening to her mother play when she was just making music for herself, not playing for them all to sing. The music made Peanut feel happy. This new house really seemed like home when her mother filled it with piano playing.

Jilly sat on the edge of a chair, watching and listening. She had never seen fingers move so fast. How did Mrs. Butterman do that? She wasn't even looking at them — her eyes were on the music on the rack. Jilly's toes tapped, and she didn't know she was doing that. She felt full of the music.

Mrs. Butterman's fingers skipped up to the high notes, then flicked back down the keyboard to the low notes. The music ended with a deep, resounding chord. "There!" She sat back. "I'm getting better at that one. I'll get it completely right one of these days."

Jilly's eyebrows lifted. How could the music be better? It had sounded perfect.

Mrs. Butterman swung around on the bench. "Did you have a good day at school?"

"Uh-huh," said Peanut, rubbing her chin on the top of Nibbsie's head.

"And are you going to introduce me to your friend?" asked Mrs. Butterman, smiling at Jilly.

Friend? Peanut and Jilly eyed each other. Then Peanut introduced Jilly. "We're working on something," she said. "And we're hungry. Is there any of that apple crisp left from dinner last night?"

"It's in the fridge," said Mrs. Butterman. "You can eat it now — if you don't mind having canned pears for dessert tonight. Help yourself.

And Jilly," she added as the girls started to leave the room, "come and see us often. You're welcome." She went back to her music.

Peanut poured milk into Snoopy glasses. She cut big squares of the apple crisp and slid them messily onto paper plates. "Paper plates are best," she explained. "You don't have to wash them."

She found puppy cookies for Nibbsie, and then they sat at the table, eating. The sound of the piano drifted into the kitchen from the living room. From time to time Peanut leaned down and offered Nibbsie a treat.

"You want to feed him?" she asked Jilly, sliding a cookie across the table.

Jilly held the cookie between two fingers. "Here, boy," she coaxed. "Come on, fella. Don't be scared."

Nibbsie approached her warily, took the cookie delicately without touching her fingers, and went back to Peanut.

"Don't feel bad," said Peanut. "He's still kind of funny with strangers. Like I told everyone, somebody was really mean to him. He's getting better, though."

Jilly turned her attention back to the apple crisp. She smacked her lips. "This is out of this world!"

Peanut eyed her. "Maybe I'll tell you how to make it even better. Maybe I'll let you in on my supersecret recipe. I don't tell just *anybody* about it."

She hopped up and got a jar of peanut butter from the cabinet behind her.

"Like this," she said. She took a forkful of the apple crisp, dabbed a bit of peanut butter on it, and lifted it to her mouth. Her eyes were closed as though the deliciousness of it was too much to bear.

Jilly watched in wonder.

Peanut opened her eyes. "Try it. You'll like it."

Jilly did and found that there was something pretty special about peanut butter-apple crisp.

Running feet sounded on the back porch. The door banged open and Peanut's older sister Maggie exploded into the kitchen. She dropped her books on a chair.

"I got here just in time, I see," she said, her

eyes on the pan of apple crisp. "Before you ate it all."

"Wasn't going to eat it all," said Peanut.

Maggie saw the peanut butter jar and rolled her eyes. "You aren't ruining this great dessert with peanut butter!" She said *peanut butter* as though it was something gross. "And you're doing it in front of somebody!" She glanced at Jilly.

"I'm not ruining it," Peanut said good-naturedly. "It's just a way to make the last bites taste different."

Maggie groaned and helped herself to the apple crisp.

"Finished?" Peanut asked Jilly. "Come on."

Jilly followed her upstairs, thinking. Peanut's sister sure was a lot like her brother Jerry. Jerry the Prune! He always said bad things the minute he saw her. Was a prune sister better or worse than a prune brother?

"That's my room," said Peanut, pointing down the upstairs hall. "But first let's look at my oldest sister Ceci's room. Ceci's in high school." She turned into a room that held a

31

white four-poster bed covered with a shell-pink spread. Small pillows of several shades of rose were scattered on the bed.

Jilly's eyes were wide. "I feel like I'm standing in a magazine picture. This is the prettiest bedroom I ever saw. But," she said uneasily, remembering Maggie, "won't she care if we're in here?"

Peanut shook her head. "Not if we don't mess with her stuff. Ceci's so pretty, she could be on TV. And she's nice, too."

"Well, I'm glad you think so," said a laughing voice. The prettiest girl Jilly had ever seen stood in the doorway. Even with her head wrapped in a big towel, she was pretty. "Who's your buddy?" she asked, coming into the room and ruffling Peanut's hair.

Peanut told her Jilly's name. Ceci shook Jilly's hand and looked right at her and smiled and her dimples showed. She made Jilly feel as though she was the nicest thing that had happened to Ceci that day.

"Can we look at your bangle bracelets?" asked Peanut.

Ceci talked with them for quite a long time.

She let them try on the bracelets and dabbed cologne on their noses and said they could take her autograph album to look at.

"Your sister really is the prettiest real-life girl I ever saw," said Jilly as she followed Peanut to her own room.

"I hope I grow up to be exactly like her," said Peanut. She didn't add, "and not like old Maggie."

She turned into her room. "Maggie and I used to share, but we don't anymore. Maggie's got her own room upstairs. She wanted a waterbed, but my mom said the floor wasn't strong enough to hold it. So she got a brass day bed. I'll get to pick my own furniture when I'm twelve, too. But these bunk beds are okay."

They curled up on the window seat to look at the autograph book and ask each other more questions.

"What's the best thing that ever happened to you?"

"Who's your favorite singer?"

"Do you like roller coasters?"

"Do you like boys?" They giggled a lot over that one.

# CHAPTER
## 5

"Now remember," said Miss Kraft, "you are to give me your animal reports before you go home today. And you are not to put your names on them."

Hands flew up around the room. "If we don't put our names on them, how will you know who did them?" asked Courtney.

"Elementary, my dear Watson," said Miss Kraft. "I'll write your animals on my list next to your names when you give me your papers. Don't worry — I won't mix them up. I know everyone's handwriting — not to mention spelling," she added, making a wry face.

Kevin looked puzzled. "Why did she call Courtney 'Watson'?"

"That's what Sherlock Holmes always said to his sidekick," explained David.

Kevin had heard of Sherlock Holmes. "Oh." But then he thought of something else. "But she said 'elementary.' I thought that meant school." Things were sometimes hard for Kevin to understand.

"Dumbo," muttered Ollie. "What a Dumbo."

David swung around and glared at Ollie. Then he explained about "elementary" to Kevin. "It's a big word for 'easy,'" he said. "Like, in elementary school we learn the easy stuff. Later it gets harder."

Kevin looked as if he wondered how things could get any harder than they were right then.

Everybody in class had started talking.

Miss Kraft smacked her desk with the book she was holding. "Quiet down, everyone."

There was instant silence.

"Work on your reports now. Pilgrims, let's get over to the reading corner."

The Pilgrims were readers who needed extra help. Everybody knew that. Kevin and a few of the other kids drifted after Miss Kraft to the sunny corner under the windows.

Nate settled down, working hard, a worried frown on his face, his tongue poking out of the corner of his mouth. He was writing slowly and with great care.

Ollie leaned over to look, bumping Nate's elbow.

Hastily Nate covered his paper with his arm. "Hey! You made me mess up my paper. And anyway — you're not supposed to know which animal I am."

"All right already," said Ollie in an aggrieved tone. "Don't be such a wimp."

Nate gave a despairing sigh and pulled a fresh sheet of paper out of his notebook.

Jilly looked across the rows at Peanut. Peanut just happened to be looking back at her.

"After school?" Jilly mouthed the words without making a sound. "My house?"

Peanut understood and nodded. "Lots of questions," she mouthed back at Jilly.

Then they got to work on their animal reports. They had spent a lot of time with each other in the past week, interviewing each other. But they had not told each other what animals they had chosen. Nobody was supposed to tell — that was part of the project.

*I am a peregrine falcon*, wrote Jilly. *I fly high in the sky.* Hey! That was poetry. She sat back and read it, pleased with herself. Then she continued writing.

*Sometimes I hold my wings out stiff and slide down the wind. Then I flap, flap, flap my wings. I go up, up, up. Pretty soon I slide down the wind again. That's how I play.*

Her chin propped on her hand, she thought for a while. *I can see everything*, she wrote at last. *I can fly anywhere. A bird is freer than any other animal.* She went on to write about eggs and baby falcons.

At her desk, Peanut was working hard, too. *I am a dolphin*, she wrote. *Us dolphins have more fun than anybody. That's why we've got these big smiles on our faces. We swim and swoop around in the waves and it's like the whole ocean belongs to us.*

She had to think for quite a while after she wrote that. Writing was hard work. She frowned a lot and doodled a picture of a dolphin on her work sheet.

*I saw dolphins at Marineland once*, she wrote. Then she stopped and scrubbed that out with her eraser. It sounded like a girl talking, not a dolphin.

She began again. *Some of my dolphin cousins live in this dinky pool in a place called Ma-*

*rineland. I saw them.* She had to erase the last three words. Girl, again — not dolphin talking. *They saw a kid watching them one day. Everyone is good to my cousins. But it would be better if they had the whole ocean to swim in like I do.*

There was lots more. She wrote about how dolphins breathed air. The best part was about dolphins saving a sailor who was drowning. They pushed him above the waves so he could breathe.

When the bell rang, everybody lined up at Miss Kraft's desk to give her their animal papers. Then they shrugged into their jackets and backpacks and headed for home.

Jilly looked sideways at Peanut. "I bet I'll be able to pick out your animal," she said.

Peanut didn't think so. She shook her head. "Not in a billion years."

Jilly insisted. "It will be an animal that's just like you."

That gave Peanut something to think about. Maybe she was sort of like a dolphin, always having so much fun. "Well, if that's so, I'll be able to pick out your paper, too. Your animal will tell me all about you, too."

Jilly looked startled. Did she want everybody to know all about her?

"Listen," said Peanut. "I've got this great question for you. Do you put on your right shoe or your left shoe first?"

Looking down at her feet, trying to remember what she did every morning, Jilly thought for a while. "Left," she said at last.

"Me, too," said Peanut, looking surprised.

Jilly was puzzled. "But what does that mean?"

Peanut blinked. She had only thought of the question, not what it meant. But she came up with an answer quickly. "People who put on their left shoe first have more fun than people who don't." She said it in a very positive voice.

"You made that up!" said Jilly.

Peanut put on a wise look. "I did, huh? Well, you just watch. You'll see for yourself."

Left foot first. . . . Jilly resolved to watch barefoot people whenever she could. She didn't know that Peanut had just made up her mind to do the very same thing.

# CHAPTER
## 6

■ ■ ■ ■ ■ ■ ■ ■ ■ ■ ■ ■ ■ ■ ■

"We're a three-cat family," Jilly explained, standing in the front hall cuddling Bumptious while Peanut knelt on the floor trying to make friends with Bonkers. Dr. Blankenstein had leaped up onto the coat rack.

Bonkers permitted herself to be picked up. "They sure are different from each other," said Peanut. "I mean, this one's a calico and yours is gray."

"Watch out for Dr. Blankenstein," said Jilly. "He jumps on people's shoulders from up there."

Peanut scooted backwards, eyeing the yellow cat draped over the ornately carved top of the coat rack.

"Oh, he's not mean," Jilly reassurred her. "He just tries to be friendly. The thing is, you've got to like his kind of friendly."

A door slammed somewhere at the back of the house. The yellow cat landed on the floor with a thump and ran toward the kitchen.

"I guess my brother Jerry just came in," said Jilly. "That's his cat."

The front door opened and a little boy slipped inside. " 'Bye, Mrs. Potter," he called. Then reaching up with both hands on the handle, he pushed the door shut.

He came directly to Peanut. "Excuse me," he said matter-of-factly, "but that's my cat you're holding."

"Oh. Sorry," said Peanut, letting the patchy cat slip into his arms.

"That's okay," he said. "Miss me, Bonk?" he asked, holding the cat against his cheek.

Peanut looked inquiringly at Jilly.

"My little brother," said Jilly. "Jackie, this is Peanut."

"Hi," said Jackie. "You can hold Bonkers

sometime," he added kindly. "Only I have to hug him first when I come home from Mrs. Potter's."

He was, thought Peanut, the neatest little kid she had ever seen, all kindness and sweetness. His eyes were enormous and surprisingly brown under his blond hair.

"Come on upstairs, everybody," a pleasant baritone voice called from somewhere high in the house. "Jerry, bring another bottle of milk from the kitchen."

"That's my dad," Jilly explained. "He's always here. He's an artist and he works upstairs in his studio. Maybe my mom will be here today. But maybe she won't. She's a teacher and sometimes she has to stay after school."

Footsteps pounded through the living room. A boy, bigger than Peanut and Jilly, came into the hall holding a half-gallon bottle of milk in one arm and the yellow cat in the other. "Greetings, flea-face," he said to Jilly. "How many people did you scare today?"

"Not as many as you did, jug-ears," Jilly said calmly.

The boy grinned maddeningly. He didn't

even acknowledge Peanut's presence, but went up the stairs with the milk and his cat.

"Jerry's kind of a prune," Jilly explained as they climbed the stairs to the studio. "Don't mind him if he says anything terrible."

Jackie followed them, taking the steps one at a time.

"Want some help?" Peanut offered, looking back at him.

He shook his head. "I can do it by myself," he said proudly. "I'm getting better and better."

Peanut had never been anyplace like the studio at the top of the stairs. A sign from the old West hung on the wall facing the stairs. It said STAGECOACH STOP. An old rifle, longer than Peanut was tall, was mounted on another wall, and beside it hung a big-brimmed cowboy hat and a silver sheriff's star. A pair of boots with spurs was in a glass case on a table. The boots were shiny, but they had creases and bumps in them, made by someone's feet a long time ago.

"Well," said Mr. Matthews, catching sight of Peanut. "Company. We're always glad to

46

have company. It's a civilizing influence after school — definitely civilizing."

Jilly let Bumptious leap to the floor and introduced Peanut. Mr. Matthews stood up from the chair behind his artist's board to shake her hand just as though she were a grown-up lady.

" 'Peanut,' you say? Seems to me I have something around here to celebrate your first visit to the Matthews *ménage*." With much clattering and clanking, he poked around in a low cabinet next to the drawing board.

Peanut followed Jilly to a low table set in front of low square windows and watched as she set out snacks and Jerry poured milk. As they settled down to munch, Mr. Matthews came to the table holding a round tin box. "I knew this would come in handy one of these days. I did a job for the Nuts To You people a while back."

Jilly leaned forward to see what was in the tin. Her father's clients were always sending things to the studio for him to draw. Sometimes the things were big and he sent them back later. But other times the things were small and he could keep them — like this box of peanut brittle. She grinned. It was exactly right today.

Mr. Matthews passed it around the table and everybody took a piece. Peanut remembered her manners and was careful to take only a medium-size piece. But Jerry dug around in the box and found the very biggest piece.

"To Peanut," said Mr. Matthews, holding up a glossy, lumpy piece of the candy before biting into it.

Peanut had to laugh. What a nice man Jilly's father was!

"To Peanut," said Jilly and Jackie, imitating him. Jerry ignored her.

Later Jilly showed her around the studio. There were drawers and drawers of big sheets of paper and paints and colored marking pens.

"You mean you can just come up here any old time and draw pictures whenever you feel like it?" Peanut asked in wonder as they went downstairs.

"Well, not exactly," said Jilly, hopping down the steps, her arms out as though she were flying. "If my dad has an important job or a deadline, we have to be quiet and not bother him. And we can't use his best brushes and some other things. But there's all kinds of stuff we can use."

Peanut looked envious and stepped aside quickly as Bumpy skittered past her down the stairway.

"It's pretty neat," Jilly admitted as she turned into her room on the second floor. She loved to draw and paint.

Peanut stopped before a picture of a gray, green-eyed cat that was pinned to the bulletin board. "What a great picture of Bumpy. Did you do it?"

Jilly nodded. "The tail's wrong, though — she wouldn't keep it still." She stroked Bumpy's head. "You've got to learn to sit still when I paint you, Bumps."

Peanut watched. "She's almost the exact color of your eyes." Then she added, "Have you seen the way cats squeeze their eyes shut when you pat their heads?"

Jilly went to the mirror to check that out, watching as she stroked Bumpy's head. Sure enough, the gray cat's eyes did squinch shut.

"I always knew that," she said wonderingly, "but I never thought about it before."

Then they got down to serious talk.

"When are you going to write about me?"

"Tonight."

"Me, too."

"Listen, I've got another question. If you could be anyone in one of the fairy tales, who would you be?"

"The girl who kissed the beast. She was really nice. Who would you be?"

"Rumpelstiltskin."

"You would not!"

"Would, too. This is only pretend. I always waited for that part in the story where he stamped his foot so hard he stamped himself right into the ground."

"Listen. Here's another question. If you couldn't be a girl, would you like to be a boy?"

"A boy! Not in a billion years."

"I like being a girl."

"So do I."

# CHAPTER
## 7

■▼■▼■■▼■▼■■▼■■▼■■▼■■▼■■▼■■▼■

The class was divided into two teams, the Bees and the Jays. They did that by covering their eyes and taking pictures of bees or jays out of Miss Kraft's hat. The winning team was going to get to play a joke on the losers.

Miss Kraft had taped the animal reports to the chalkboard. The teams read the reports and tried to guess who had written which — which animal each of them had chosen to be.

The Jays were in one corner, making up their list of guesses, and the Bees were in another. Each team had half the list right, of course, because team members could tell each other what animals they had chosen. But the rest of the list? There was much muttering and whispering.

"Listen! The elephant's gotta be — " "Shhh!" "They'll hear!" Mumbles followed from the Jays' corner.

Giggles came from the Bees' corner. "They won't get it." "Don't look at them — they'll guess." "I bet the kangaroo is — " "Quiet!"

"Time," Miss Kraft called. "Finish up your lists and give them to me."

Groans filled the room.

Elena and Courtney, who were writing the lists, hurried to finish. They gave the papers to Miss Kraft, who began checking them against her own list.

Peanut and Jilly looked at each other from their corners. Jilly was a Bee; Peanut, a Jay. Which team was going to win? What terrible trick was going to be played on the losers?

"Welllllll. . . ." Miss Kraft looked up, drawing out the word.

"Tell us, tell us." "Who won?"

"The Bees got the most right."

"Yea!" "All ri-ight!" "I told you we'd win."

The Bees slapped each other's hands in congratulations.

"Awwww." "Did you count right?" "We wuz robbed." "Booo." The boo was very soft.

The Jays did not take losing lightly. They watched nervously as the Bees whispered their plans to Miss Kraft. Elvis was doing most of the talking. But Jilly was laughing and talking, too.

Her head on one side, Miss Kraft listened. After a while, she gave her permission with a nod.

The Jays exchanged looks. Here it came.

The Bees huddled together like a football team, talking in low voices. At last they turned and faced the Jays.

"Line up against the chalkboard," said Kevin, who looked proud to be on the winning team.

"We're going to give you a singing lesson," said Elvis. He started to laugh.

"Hey, hang onto yourself. Don't come apart now," said one of the Bees.

Elvis gulped and pulled himself together, looking as though he was going to choke.

The Jays crowded to the front of the room.

"Half of you stand at that side of the board," directed Nate, pointing to his right, "and the other half stand on that side." He motioned to his left.

There was more moving around as the Jays tried to figure out how many people made half.

"Okay now," said Elvis. "You guys" — he pointed to the right — "sing the way I do. Awwww," he sang in a low voice.

"Awwww," sang half the Jays.

"Now you" — Emmy pointed to the left — "sing Eeeeee." Her voice was high. "Eeeee."

"Eeeeee," came from the left. "Eeeee."

David stepped forward. "I'm the conductor. Ahem. When I point to you, sing." He pointed to the right, to the left.

"Awwww."

"Eeeee."

"Faster," he called, pointing wildly. Right, left, right, left.

"Awww." "Eeee."

Somehow, before they quite figured out how it happened, the Jays found themselves singing "Eeeee-awwww ... Eeeee-awwww ... Eeeee-awwww."

Peanut was the first to catch on. She broke down, clutching her sides.

Elvis joined her. "You sound just like . . . just like — " He couldn't finish, he was laughing so hard.

"Donkeys!" Ollie exploded. "You made us sound like a bunch of donkeys." He looked outraged.

But nobody else cared as they leaned helplessly against each other, doubled over. Even Miss Kraft was laughing.

The bell jangled over their laughter.

"Polly . . . Jillian," Miss Kraft called, "please stay for a few minutes."

Ollie stopped next to Jilly's desk. There were still traces of laughter around her eyes and mouth. "Meat Head," he grumbled. "I bet that was your idea, you being so smart and everything."

Peanut heard him. Her eyes shot sparks. "Don't you dare call Jilly Meat Head, Oliver Burke. Don't you dare!"

Ollie looked confused. "Why should you care, Fat Stuff?"

Jilly's face got red. She pushed her face close

to Ollie's. He backed away. "Don't you call Peanut fat, Oliver Burke. She's not fat. She's just . . . just . . . pleasingly plump. I'm never going to help you find anything in the encyclopedia again, Oliver Burke. So there!"

"Girls," Ollie muttered disgustedly. "Girls! Don't know a joke when they hear one." He headed out the door.

# CHAPTER
## 8

The room was, after all the laughter, suddenly very quiet. Peanut and Jilly leaned against Miss Kraft's desk.

"Well?" she asked. "Did you do your 'I am' reports?"

Peanut and Jilly put them on her desk.

Miss Kraft held up her hands, palms out. She shook her head. "I don't have to see them. But I wonder if you would like to share them with each other."

Shyly, the girls exchanged their papers.

" 'My name is Polly Butterman,' " read Peanut. " 'But I've got this really great nickname — Peanut. I talk a lot and I laugh a lot and I make everybody else talk and laugh and feel good. My hair is shiny brown and my eyes are shiny brown, too, like acorns. I've got the nicest big sister of anybody in the world. My other sister is terrible, but maybe she will grow out of it. I've got a puppy named Nibbsie, and I'm very kind to him. I used to live in Minneapolis, but now I live here and I like it. I'm going to stay here forever.' "

She looked up, starting to say, "Why, that's just like me." But she saw that Jilly was reading.

" 'My name is Jillian Matthews,' " read Jilly. " 'My hair is a beautiful yellow color. My eyes match my gray cat. I'm kind of quiet and shy around people I don't know, but when I get to know someone I'm not shy. I laugh a lot. I've got a darling little brother and I've got a terrible big brother. He doesn't know how lucky he is to have me. My friend Peanut Butterman says she is lucky.' "

Jilly looked up, her eyes shining. She liked the friend part, and she wished she had written that about Polly.

Miss Kraft was watching them. "Lesson concluded," she said. "You don't have to interview each other anymore."

"But I want to," said Jilly.

"Me, too," said Peanut.

"I don't think I have to say another word," said Miss Kraft. "Run along now."

The girls started to leave.

"Oh, just a minute," called Miss Kraft. Turning, she picked up the bowls Peanut and Jilly had left on her desk last week. "I like blue," she said, "and I like red. What would the world be like without blue skies and red valentines? Neither is better than the other. We need them both to be happy."

Peanut and Jilly hugged their bowls as they went down the steps of Louisa May Alcott School.

"We both hate dancing lessons," said Peanut as they turned toward home.

"We both put on our left shoe first," said Jilly. She glanced sideways at Peanut. "But I don't believe that about people having more fun."

"But haven't we had more fun this week?" asked Peanut.

It was true. They had.

Jilly turned her blue bowl, admiring it. It was the best bowl she had ever made. She held it out. "I'd like you to have my bowl," she said.

Peanut held out her red bowl. "This is for you."

They stopped at the corner, waiting to cross the street, holding their bowls.

"Valentines. This is always going to make me think of valentines."

"This will always make me think of blue skies."

"Always."

"Forever."